Walter the White Crayon

Hey, that's me!

By Dawn Brock & Katie Alusa

Dedicated to anyone who has ever felt like they were as useful as a white crayon.

ISBN: 978-1-7361052-0-7

Printed in the USA

Walter couldn't believe it; his box had *finally* been opened!

Walter had been waiting for this day his whole life.

This was the day that a child would use **HIM** to draw!

When a child reached for his box,
Walter looked up excitedly.

Would he be the first crayon chosen?

No. The hand moved
over him and picked up
his sibling, blue crayon.

Walter was disappointed, but he
was not worried.
He knew his time would come.

Months passed, and not one child
chose to draw with Walter.
So many children drew
apples with red crayon...

...and oceans with
blue crayon.

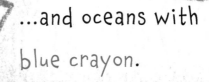

Walter lost count of the
number of frogs drawn by
green crayon...

and sunflowers by
yellow crayon.

Yet, Walter drew nothing....

One day, a little
girl picked him up.

Walter was so excited.
His time had come!

However, his smile
quickly disappeared
as the girl bit
into Walter before
throwing him aside in
disgust. **Yuck!**

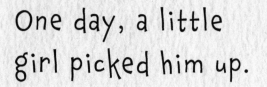

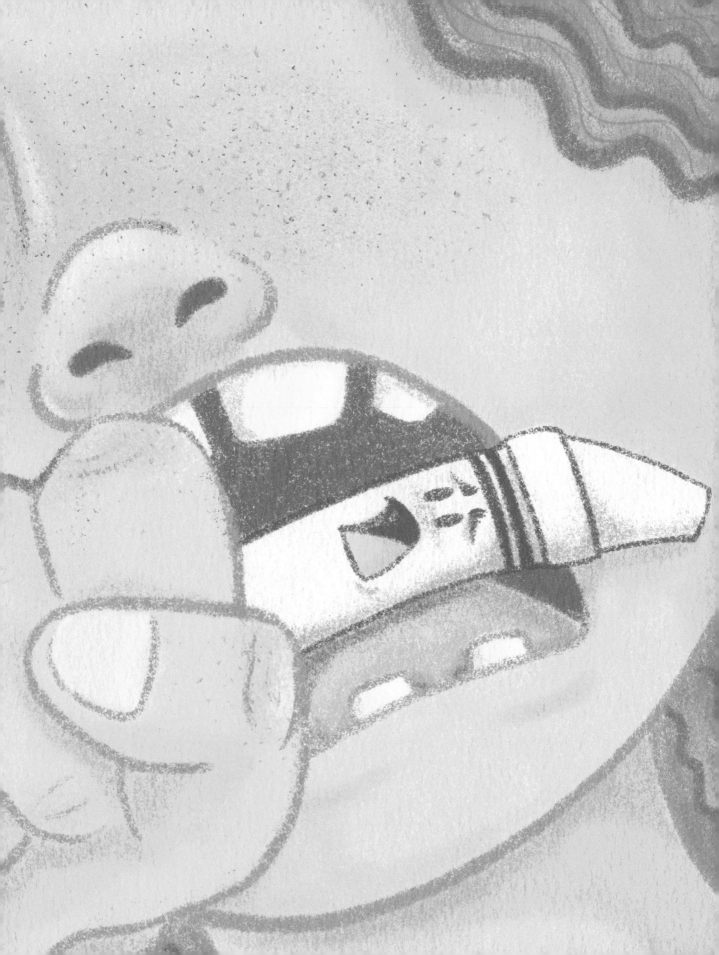

Walter watched as all of his siblings became shorter and shorter.

They brought happiness to the children who used them while Walter could not.

Walter finally accepted that no child would ever want to draw with him.

He felt useless.

Who needed a white crayon?

No one.

One day a little girl brought something new,

Black paper.

She picked Walter up and began to draw.

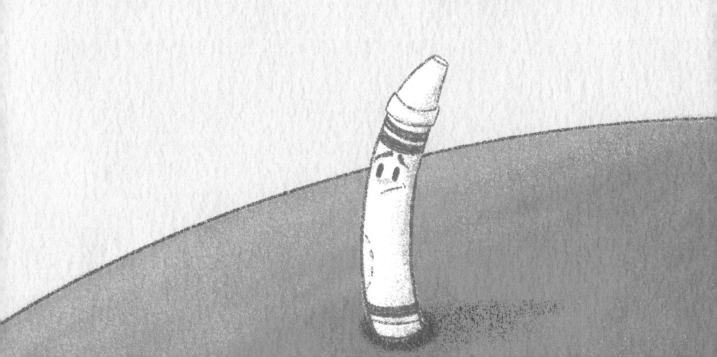

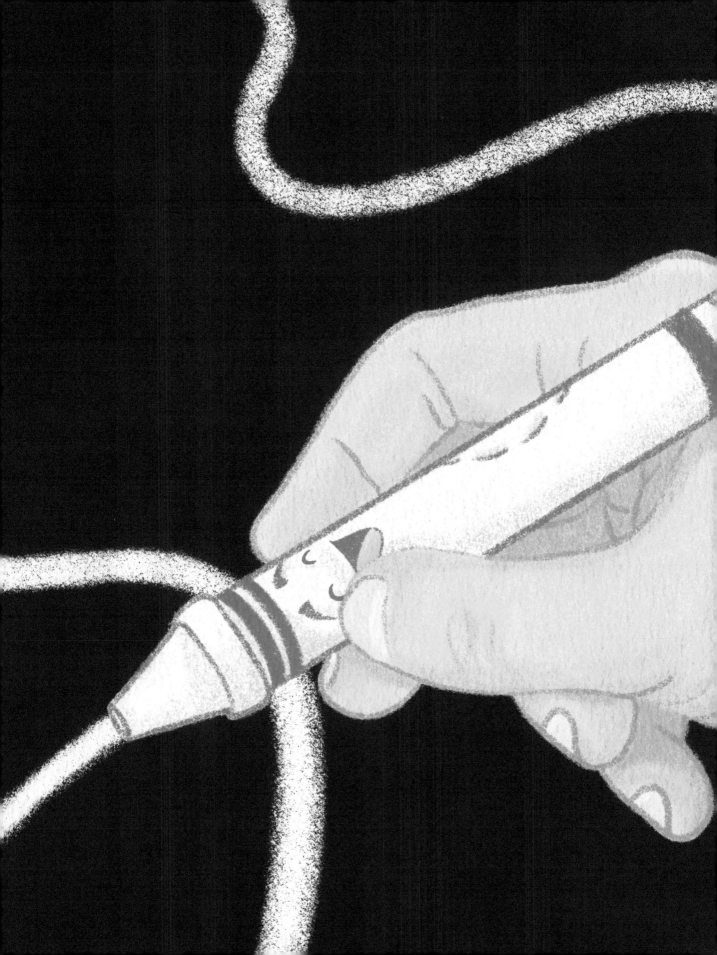

The girl drew unicorns...

...swans...

...clouds...

...polar bears...

...and much more.
She had an endless imagination.

The girl colored with Walter
all day, sparking the interest
of the children around her.

Walter smiled as he quickly grew shorter.

Finally, the day he had always dreamt of had arrived!

He was so happy he thought he would burst.

At the end of the day, Walter's siblings gathered around him and looked up at their creations, none of which shined brighter than **Walter's.**

About the Author & Illustrator

Dawn Brock

Dawn Brock loves all things books and reading. She has dreamed of being a published author for years. Walter has been her brainchild for years, and she is proud and grateful for him to be her first published work. Dawn has a bachelor's degree in English and is currently studying to get her master's degree. She is so grateful for the opportunity to work with Katie Alusa. Dawn has loved Walter for many years, and she hopes you grow to love him too.

To find out more, visit thisgirlwrites.com

Katie Alusa

Katie Alusa is a Graphic Designer who loves all things art. She has thoroughly enjoyed venturing out of her comfort zone and illustrating Walter's story. Katie grew up in Utah and in Nottingham England, drawing and designing at any chance she got. She graduated from Dixie State University with a degree in Graphic Design. She began working on Walter as a senior in college and has learned a great deal from him. Now she lives in Utah with her husband, the wonderful Malachi Alusa.

To see more of her work, please visit alusadesign.com

Special thanks to Rachel Ramsay, Daisy Olivares, Addi, Boston, Ellie, Peter, Miles, Gunnar, Erin, and Zoe, who's passion inspired us.

Thank you for your support!

Printed in the USA
CPSIA information can be obtained
at www.ICGtesting.com
LVHW060853170923
758433LV00002B/75